DISCARD

For the sea, so beautiful when
the moon smiles at its hair.
Cathy

General Manager: Gauthier Auzou
Senior Editor: July Zaglia
English Version Editor: Nelson Yomtov
Layout: Annaïs Tassone
Original title: *La gardienne des océans*
© Éditions Auzou, Paris (France),
2011 (English version)
ISBN: 978-2-7338-1941-8

Printed and bound in China, 2011

The Legend of Elinea
The Guardian of the Oceans

An ecological tale by Cathy Delanssay

An ancient legend tells us of a sea goddess that reigns over the depths of all the seas. Since the beginning of time, she has been the mother of all marine creatures, whom she loves and protects. Respected in days gone by, she has since been forgotten… but her legend has not completely died.

She is called Elinea, the guardian of the oceans.

Way out at sea, far from the continent, there was an island,
lulled by the swell and the currents of the ocean.
Fishermen used to live on this small piece
of land, in their houses with blue roofs.

The inhabitants lived there happily,
far away from the big towns.

They lacked nothing thanks to the abundance of fish and
golden fields that spread out, like a cover, over their fertile land.

The members of Bastian's family
had been fisherman from one generation
to the next.
Every day, Bastian and his brothers
would go out to sea to catch the necessary
amount of fish to meet the needs
of their fellow villagers.

The fishermen would sing under the caress
of the sun. They were accompanied by the dolphins,
the sea turtles and the seagulls, which, attracted
by the smell of the fish, would fly close
to the fishermen's boats.

Life was simple and wonderful, and nothing
could tarnish this bliss.

But one day, a big, dark boat was spotted just off the coast.

These ocean pirates, who were so dreaded by the fishermen,
dragged the seabed with their immense fishing nets.

They injured the dolphins, the turtles and the fish, which were
taken by surprise by the sharp-edged mesh of the pirates' nets!

They were of no interest to the poachers so they
would be thrown back into the sea, either injured… or dead…

The poachers captured many, many fish.
And soon there was a shortage of fish on Bastian's island.

And so the years passed . . .
Few people were concerned about the fate of the islanders,
And even fewer cared about the inhabitants of the ocean.

Sorrow overcame the waters . . .
And the sea's dress turned from blue to red in mourning.

In the depths of the sea, a force was disrupting the tides.
Elinea, the guardian of the oceans, was muttering angrily!

"You are irresponsible!" she cried to the pirates.
"Is this how you thank the sea for all that it offers you?"

Full of anger and brandishing her trident,
Elinea spread out her hair, which made the sea toss and turn!
Furious winds blew, and rain fell down in sheets!
A sea storm beat down upon the pirates' boat.

But the huge ship was very strong. The storm could not stop it.

Elinea's anger was so great that her hair grew and grew, until it got caught in the immense nets of the pirates ships.

Elinea lost her trident in the powerful waves, and without her powers . . .

Elinea was captured by the pirates!

Little by little, the sea changed.
The pattern of the tides were disturbed.
And the fish, which strayed in the depths of
the sea, got lost in this world without Elinea.

Their mother -- the guardian of the oceans --
was no longer there to rock them
with her sweet lullabies.
The fish could no longer snuggle up
in her arms and play with her hair.

The pirates were proud of their exceptional catch of Elinea.
They organized a secret auction to sell her off to the highest bidder.
The pirates invited the greatest collectors of the world's most
extraordinary creatures to attend the auction.

The auction was to be held
on a small, secluded island.
It was Bastian's island.

One morning, while he was out walking,
Bastian heard some singing coming
from the old, abandoned mill.
It was no ordinary singing but rather a sad lament,
like a prayer.

He approached and was astounded!
A huge creature was chained up in a fish tank!
It was Elinea!

The goddess, twenty time the size of a man,
spun around in circles in her small tank.
She was distressed and felt helpless being
in a space that was far too small for her.
Fish appeared from her coral skin and kissed
her to comfort her.
They gave her small, sweet kisses on her arms,
her neck and her face.
But the guardian of the oceans still remained
sad and angry.

The pirates had hung a sign on the fish tank
that read:

"For Sale to the Highest Bidder."

Bastian understood what was going to happen to Elinea.
Feeling sorry for the guardian of the oceans,
he walked up to the her fish tank and spoke to her.

"Who are you?" he asked gently.
"I am Elinea, the ocean mother and guardian,"
she replied sadly.
Bastian shivered.
He understood that Elinea's capture was the cause
of the disaster happening in the sea.
He asked her how he could help.

"My trident can be found in the place where
the sun sets and the moon rises," she said.
"Thanks to its powers, you will be able
to make your way toward the sea and
free me from my chains. I could then
be free by the next tide!"

Bastian was afraid!
Although he lived a simple,
ordinary life, he courageously
accepted Elinea's astonishing challenge.
His love for the sea was
sincere and true!

When night fell, the sun embraced the moon
with its last rays, leaving the waves to bathe
in a soft shade of orange.

Bastian observed the sea in his boat, ready to cast off.
When the moon was at its brightest, he saw light rising
on the horizon.

Just as quickly, he set off!
He made haste, sailing through the winds and
over the currents.
Then he boldly dived into the depths
of the unknown watery world!

Bastian swam effortlessly into the deep
and silent universe, which was inhabited
by plants lulled by the flowing currents.
A strange world lay before him.
This world worried him one moment
and terrified him the next.
Suddenly, he felt a shortage of air …

His eyelids became heavy,
and everything turned dark
and freeing cold.

Bastian weakened.
He continued to drift further
into the watery depths, and
as the last air bubbles escaped
from his mouth, he was carried
away by the currents . . .
and he disappeared.

It was at this moment that the fish started gathering
and dancing around Bastian in a strange way.

A small, golden fish lightly brushed against
his mouth and he regained consciousness.

His lungs filled with air and his body warmed up again;
Bastian was able to breathe once more!

Once again, he was overcome with a fear of the unknown.
But now Bastian thought of the fate of the seas and
the one who could save it -- Elinea. He had to complete
his mission at all costs!

So, Bastian continued his descent among the fish,
which guided him toward the dark, blue depths.

Deeper and deeper into
the dark world where legends
are born -- in a forest of seaweed
and coral -- Elinea's trident
revealed itself!

It proudly stood there, brightly shining!
Bastian was surrounded by the power
of the trident. Its glowing aura scattered spots
of light throughout the water and onto the scales
of the nearby fish.
Never before had Bastian seen such light ...
nor had he ever felt such force when he grabbed
the precious object!

Elinea's singing could then
be heard in the vast depths.
The trident sparkled!

Suddenly, Bastian was pulled by the trident
to the water's surface at an incredible speed.
In moments, he reached the shore, shaken
by his journey into the sea. He gathered
his spirits and held tightly onto the trident,
which began to shine even more and more!

Bastian ran to the abandoned mill where
Elinea was being held captive in her fish tank.
Brandishing the trident, Bastian unleashed
thunderbolts that burrowed into the earth,
breaking the tank apart and turning Elena's
chains to dust.
Elinea shook her long hair and stretched:
she was beautiful and powerful once again.

She was free.

Bastian handed the trident back
to the goddess who smiled at him tenderly.

The tide bowed in respect and then
took Elinea back to the deep of the sea,
where she would find her fish again.

The water caressed her skin and smoothed
out her hair; she regained her force which
was greater and more splendid than ever!

She cut through the currents from North to South, from East to West; the waves broke and crashed against the rocks !

An immense wave rose on the horizon!

It was so big! It was so high!

It was an insurmountable wall of water!

The pirates, who were both terrified and helpless,
fled from the ocean and left the high seas in peace.
The dark boat never returned.
And from that day, the pirates would never forget
the old legend that they would always live in fear of:

The Legend of Elinea, the guardian of the oceans.

Life returned to normal on the island with blue roofs.
The fish returned, and the fishermen sang in the sun.
The dolphins and the seagulls laughed while playfully
teasing the turtles.
And the sea was so beautiful when the moon's smile lit up its hair.
Today, Bastian still tenderly looks at the sea, clad in its sky-blue dress.

Listen to your heart, listen to the call.
Bastian is in each one of us, telling us that,
together, we can save our delicate and beautiful seas.

Seas and oceans make up 70 percent of our planet, Earth.

For countless thousands of years, the seas have provided
humans with an abundant supply of fish to eat. But today,
the situation is changing. The oceans' natural resources
are being overfished and illegal fishing by pirates is
not being sufficiently supervised.

There has been an alarming reduction in the supplies of fish,
and many species have even become extinct. Fisherman,
on whom many coastal towns depend for food supplies,
are often unable to catch enough fish to feed their neighbours.

If people do not act to stop the loss of natural resources
in Earth's waters, the oceans will be only a memory for future
generations of humans. We can all do something to help.

For more information:
http://www.greenpeace.org